What Should I Wear?

Written by Penny Lee

On a sunny day,

I wear my T-shirt.

3

On a cloudy day,

I wear my T-shirt

and my sweater.

5

On a rainy day,

I wear my T-shirt

and my sweater

and my coat.

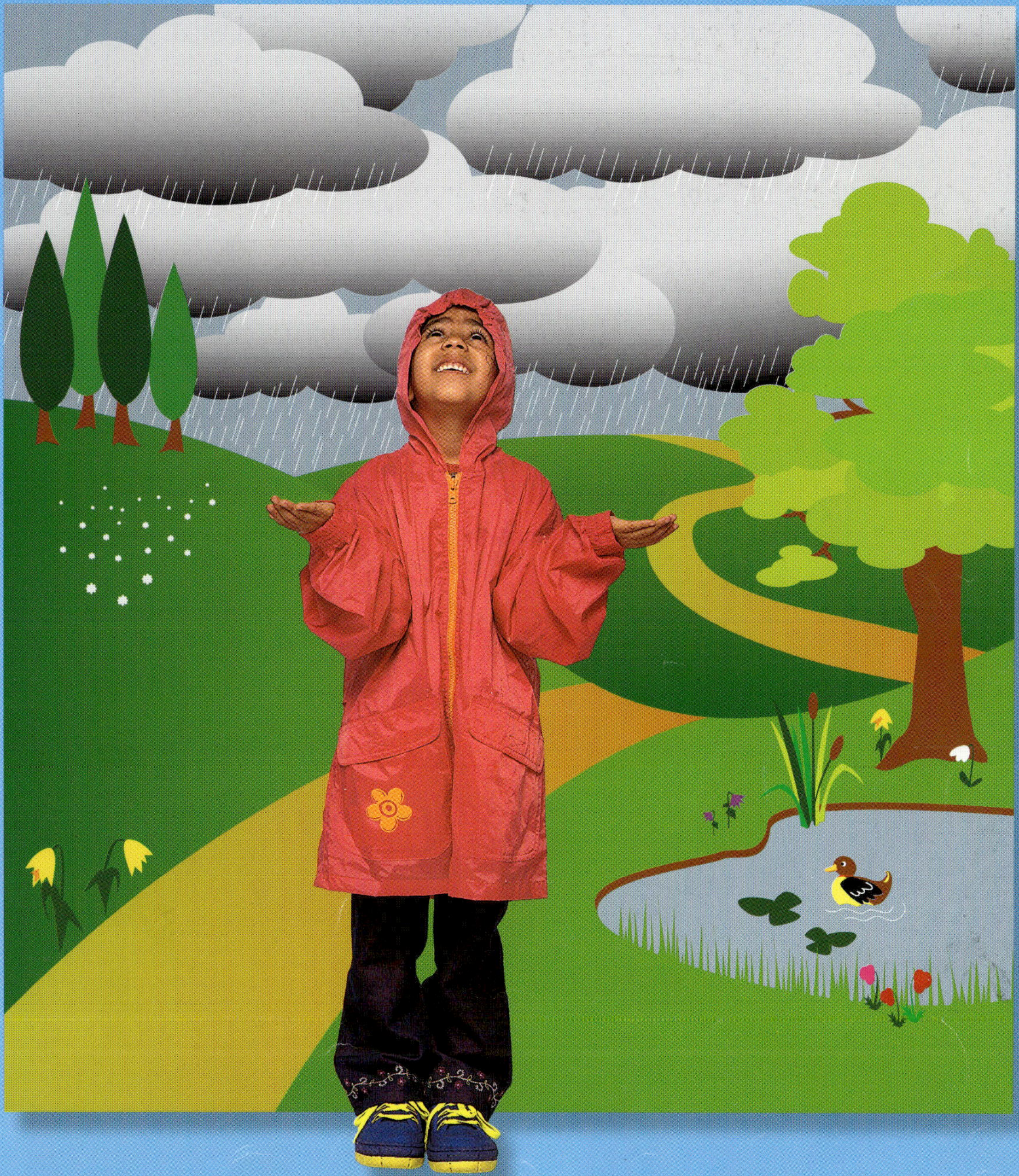

On a windy day,

I wear my T-shirt

and my sweater

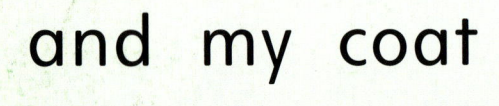

and my coat

and my scarf.

9

On a snowy day,

I wear my T-shirt

and my sweater

and my coat

and my scarf

and my gloves.

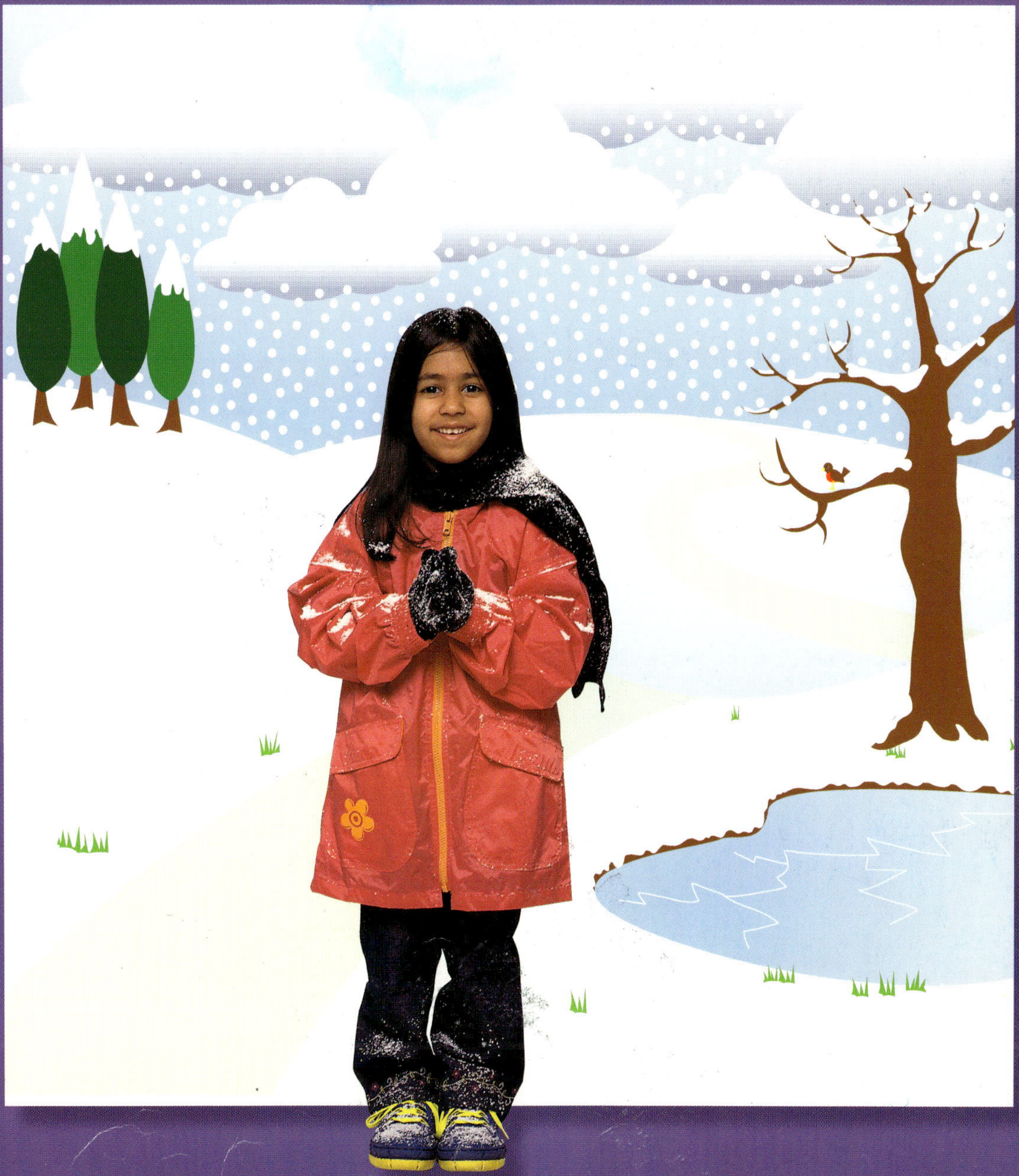

Sunny

Cloudy

Rainy

Windy

Snowy